Teachers' Pets

Paul Cookson is married and lives in Retford. He spends most of his time explaining where Retford is. He visits lots of schools performing his work and encouraging pupils and teachers to write their own poems.

PS: Retford is between Newark and Doncaster on the A1, by the way.

David Parkins has illustrated numerous books, ranging from Maths textbooks to *The Beano*. His picture books have been shortlisted for the Smarties Book Prize and the Kurt Maschler Award, and commended twice in the National Art Library Illustration Awards. He lives in Lincoln with his wife, three children and six cats.

Also available from Macmillan

TONGUE TWISTERS AND TONSIL TWIZZLERS
poems chosen by Paul Cookson

UNZIP YOUR LIPS
100 poems to read aloud
chosen by Paul Cookson

WHO RULES THE SCHOOL?
poems chosen by Paul Cookson

SANDWICH POETS

AN ODD KETTLE OF FISH
John Rice, Pie Corbett and Brian Moses

LOST PROPERTY BOX
Matt Simpson, Wes Magee and Peter Dixon

ELEPHANT DREAMS
Ian McMillan, David Harmer, Paul Cookson

Teachers' Pets

poems chosen by
Paul Cookson

illustrated by
David Parkins

MACMILLAN CHILDREN'S BOOKS

To the Staff and Pupils of
North Kesteven GM School

First published 1997 by Macmillan Children's Books
This edition produced 2001 for
The Book People Ltd,
Hall Wood Avenue,
Haydock, St Helens WA11 9UL

Created by Working Partners Limited
London W6 0HE

ISBN 0 330 34905 8

7 9 8 6

A CIP catalogue record for this book is available from
the British Library.

Typeset in Bookman Old Style
Printed and bound in Great Britain by Mackays of Chatham plc, Kent

Contents

Subtraction

Our French teacher keeps snails,
But we get quite suspicious
When she tells us that keeping snails
Is simply 'so delicious!'

She also keeps pet frogs,
She says they're good for kissing,
But what we really want to know
Is why their legs are missing!

Coral Rumble

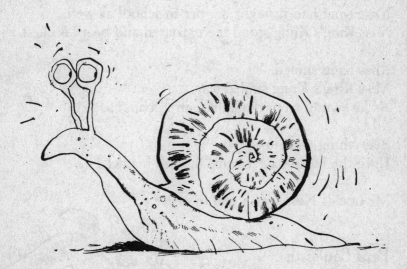

Miss King's Kong

It was our "Bring your pet to school" day . . .

Warren's wolfhound was chasing Paula's poodle
Paula's poodle was chasing Colin's cat
Colin's cat was chasing Harriet's hamster
And Harriet's hamster was chasing Benny's beetle.

Suzie's snake was trying to swallow
Freddie's frog, Percy's parrot, Rebecca's rabbit,
Belinda's bat, Gordon's goat, Peter's pig
And part of Patricia's pony

When all of a sudden everything stopped.

Miss King had brought her pet to school as well.
Miss King's Kong stood there, roared and beat his chest.

Miss King smiled.
Miss King's Kong smiled too
As he swung from the light, eating bananas.

Everything was quiet
Until the Headmaster came in with his pet . . .

Mr Lock's Ness was a real monster.

Paul Cookson

Choosing Some Suitable Pets

Big bugs and fat slugs
and blood-sucking leeches;
things that come wriggling
from plump plums and peaches;

growlers and howlers
and screamers and screechers;
vile-bodied vermin
with foulest of features;

rubbery, blubbery
deep-water species
of sea-beasts whose bodies
get washed up on beaches;

appalling things crawling
from damp nooks and niches;
slimy things climbing
where light never reaches;

hair-nits and hornets;
the grubs of such creatures . . .
It's hard to choose which pets
to get for your teachers!

Nick Toczek

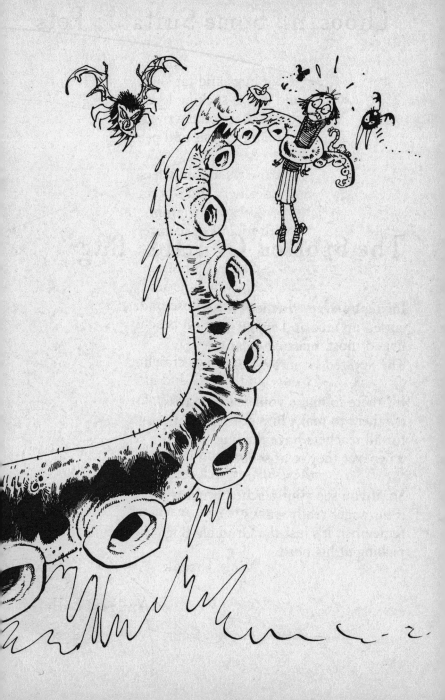

The Spotted Grumble Bug

Living up every teacher's nose,
curled up nice and snug,
lives a most amazing creature:
The Spotted Grumble Bug.

It's there to make your teacher cross,
it's there to make him cruel,
for all teachers have the bug
whenever they're at school.

So, if you see your teacher twitch,
if his anger really shows,
remember, it's just the Grumble Bug,
picking at his nose.

Andrew Collett

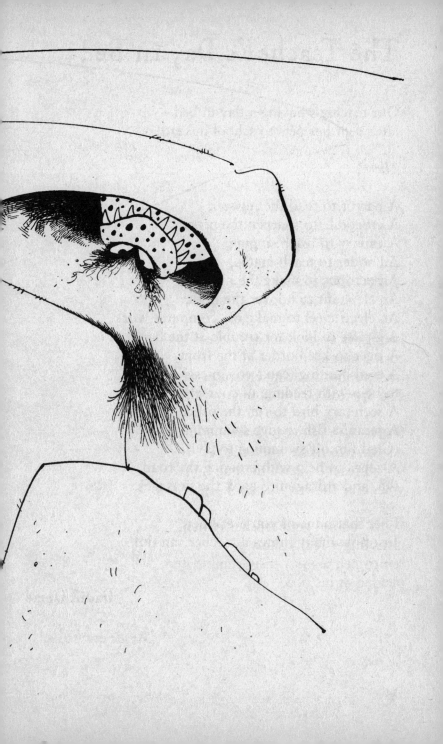

The Teacher's Day in Bed

Our teacher's having a day in bed –
She's sent her pets to school instead!

There's . . .

A parrot to read the register,
A crocodile to sharpen the pencils,
A canary to teach singing,
An adder to teach maths,
An octopus to make the ink,
An elephant to hoover the floor,
An electric eel to make the computer work,
A giraffe to look for trouble at the back,
A tiger to keep order at the front,
A reed bunting (can't you guess?
to help with reeding, of course!),
A secretary bird to run the office
A piranha fish to give swimming lessons
(Glad I'm off swimming today!),
A zebra to help with crossing the road,
Oh, and a dragon to cook the sausages.

I bet that none of you ever knew
Just how many things a teacher can do!

David Orme

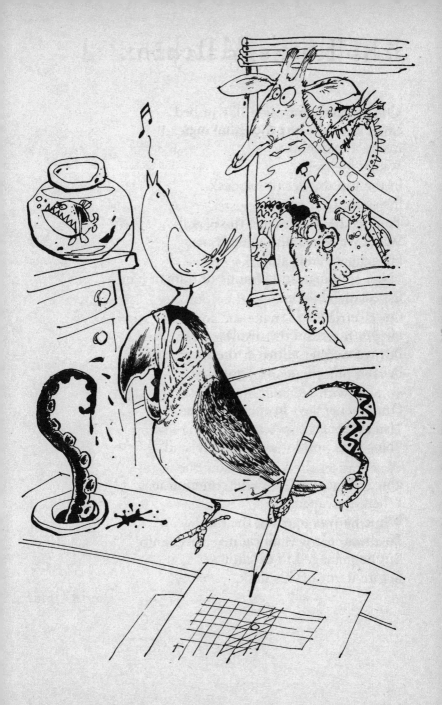

Inside Sir's Matchbox

Our teacher's pet
Lives in a nest of pencil-shavings
Inside a matchbox
Which he keeps
In the top drawer of his desk.
It's so tiny, he says,
You need a microscope to see it.
When we asked him what it ate,
He grinned and said,
"Nail clippings and strands of human hair –
Especially children's."
Once on Open Day,
He put it out on the display table,
But we weren't allowed to open the box
Because it's allergic to light.

Our teacher says his pet's unique.
"Isn't it lonely?" we asked.
"Not with you lot around," he said.

Once, there was an awful commotion
When it escaped
While he was opening the box
To check if it was all right.
But he managed to catch it
Before it got off his desk.

Since then, he hasn't taken it out so much.
He says he thinks it's hibernating at present –
Or it could be pregnant.
If it is, he says
There'll be enough babies
For us all to have one.

John Foster

Classroom Helper

Can we borrow your chipmunk, Miss?
He's such a useful pet,
So tidy and efficient,
Our best pencil sharpener yet!

Sue Cowling

Fred's Performing Flea

Fred was just a schoolteacher,
As normal as could be.
But Fred had got a special pet –
A black performing flea.

He came across it quite by chance
As it jumped off his mongrel Rover.
It leapt clear over the television
And landed on the sofa.

"Aye aye," he thought, "that's pretty good,
I've got a winner 'ere,
I'll train 'im like I train me dog –
On biscuits, chips and beer."

And so it was, day after day
Fred fed him on this diet.
And sure enough his muscles grew –
And grew and grew a riot!

Then after months of practising
The flea went for a trial –
Fred made him climb Mount Everest
Then swim the River Nile.

The flea came through without a scratch,
He never even wavered,
And as reward Fred fed him steak,
And ice-cream, brandy flavoured.

Then Fred decided it was time
To show the world his flea –
He'd even trained him to sing songs
While sipping China tea.

The people flocked from miles around,
They couldn't believe their eyes.
And against the Lions at Twickenham
He scored eleven tries!

He played against Australia
At cricket up at Lord's,
And smashed a double century
Off thirty-seven balls.

He pulverised the champion
And took the Heavyweight crown,
And just like Samson long ago
He pulled a temple down.

He raced in the Olympics
Where he won a host of medals.
(He dropped out of the cycling though –
He couldn't reach the pedals!)

He swam the great Atlantic
And then orbited the earth,
And then with weights strapped to his back
He hopped from Leeds to Perth.

He's still performing all his feats
Although he's nearly fifty,
And rumour has it, though he's aged,
Fred's flea is still quite nifty.

And one thing's sure – that years from now
In three thousand AD
They'll say the wonder of all time
Was Fred's performing flea!

Clive Webster

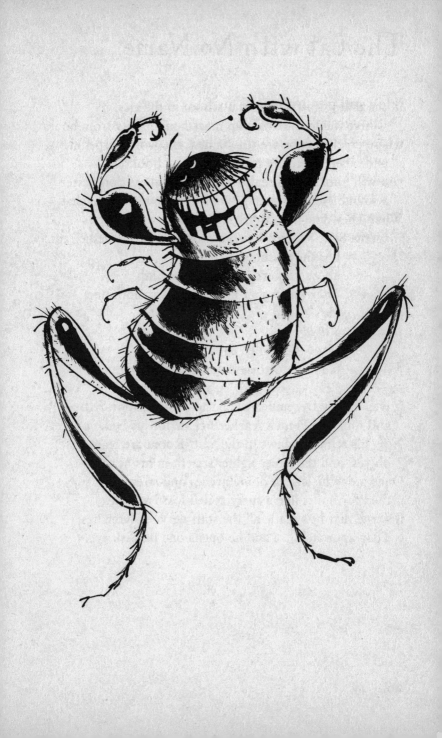

The Cat with No Name

In the dingy Staff Room of a school in the city,
    where the teachers' damp macs hang limply from hooks,
where cracked cups are tea-stained, the worn carpet gritty,
    and where there are piles of exercise books,
you will notice – at break – that the teachers don't utter
    a sound. None of them grumble and none of them chat.
Why? They dare not disturb what sleeps, fat as butter,
    on the Staff Room's best chair: one huge tortoiseshell cat.

            For the teachers
            know very well not to wake him.
            They know that he's three parts not tame.
            He's a wild cat,
            a *wild* cat,
            a not-to-be-riled cat.
            He's the tortoiseshell cat with no name.

It was drizzly December when the cat first appeared
    and took the French teacher's chair for his bed.
Now his scimitar claws in the Staff Room are feared,
    oh yes, and the street-fighter's teeth in his head.
Once a day he is seen doing arches and stretches,
    then for hours like a furry coiled fossil will lie.
It's true that he's made all the staff nervous wretches.
    They approach . . . and he opens one basilisk eye.

For the teachers
know very well not to stroke him.
They know that he'll not play the game.
He's a wild cat,
a *wild* cat,
a not-to-be-riled cat.
He's the tortoiseshell cat with no name.

The Headmistress, the teachers, and all the school's cleaners
    can't shift him with even a long-handled broom,
for the cat merely yawns, treats them all like has-beeners
    and continues to live in that dingy Staff Room.
When the French teacher tried to reclaim her armchair
    with a cat-cally, shriek-squally "Allez-vous en!",
the cat gave a hiss, clawed the lady's long hair,
    and back to Marseilles Madame Touff-Pouff has gone.
For the teachers
know very well not to irk him.
They know that he's always the same.
He's a wild cat,
a *wild* cat,
a not-to-be-riled cat.
He's the tortoiseshell cat with no name.

I once worked in that school and observed the huge creature's
    habits as I sipped my cracked cup of weak tea.
I saw how he frightened and flummoxed the teachers,
    and how – every Friday – he'd one-green-eye me.
To appease him, each day we laid out a fish dinner
    which the beast snaffled-up in just one minute flat
then returned to his chair with a smirk – the bad sinner!
    It seems there's no way to be rid of that cat.
                For the teachers
                know very well not to cross him.
                They know that he's three parts not tame.
                He's a wild cat,
                a *wild* cat,
                a not-to-be-riled cat
                (he can't bear to be smiled at).
                He's the tortoiseshell cat with no name,
                with no name.
                He's the tortoiseshell cat with no name.

        Wes Magee

Daunting Duo

Our ancient headmaster,
Grim-faced Mr Fulcher,
Has, perched on his shoulder,
A wrinkled old vulture!

With beady black eye,
And pink, balding pate,
Those two gruesome faces
Are hard to separate!

Anne Logan

Miss B's Dog

Chummie is a
brown and white
springer spaniel
who sits
by the touchline
while Miss B
sprints
back and forth
blowing
her whistle
when the team
fouls on the pitch.
Chummie
never does that.

Chris Riley

The Green Hedgehog

My teacher had a hedgehog.
It was green and looked quite ill.
Its spines were thin and pale
And it sat completely still.
Its eyes were closed so tightly,
I knew it couldn't see.
It seemed to have just lumps and bumps
Where its feet should be.
My teacher took it to the vets,
Afraid it might be dead;
The vets took just one look at it
And this is what they said:
"This sad and sorry article
Has nothing to attract us.
I'm sorry to inform you
That your hedgehog is . . . a cactus!"

Celia Warren

Anniversary

Sir still misses:
morning yawns, yawning morns
wagging words
whiskered whispers
furry verbs;
her tail told tales.

Sir still misses:
paw clauses, claw pauses
odour grammar
nose prose
dog doggerel;
a play within her play.

Sir still misses:
growl vowels, vowel growls
bush telegraph
lamp-post paragraph
tree town-crier;
scent messages sent.

Sir still misses his Jack Russell
ever so much
and so do we.

Mike Johnson

Best Pet Yet

The teachers in my school must think
they're working in a zoo.
Their classrooms feature many a creature.
Here are just a few:

Mr Lee has a chimpanzee.
It leaps about and wriggles.
It pulls his hair and bumps his chair
and gives us all the giggles.

Mrs Drake has a ten-foot snake
inside a case of glass.
When children shout she lets it out
to quieten down the class.

Mr Matt has a vampire bat
with teeth that smile and bite.
When it's time for sums it shows its gums
and helps us get them right!

Mrs Rider wears a spider
dangling from one ear.
It does no harm. It's meant to charm,
but fills us full of fear.

Mr Breeze keeps jumping fleas
in a jar on the windowsill.
I wonder why his class all cry,
"Please sir, we can't sit still."

Mrs Swish keeps angelfish.
They help to calm us down.
Their gentle glide drifts deep inside
and smoothes away each frown.

But young Miss Sweet, so nice and neat,
has the best pet there can be.
I hope she'll get no other pet,
for neat Miss Sweet has ME!

Tony Mitton

Changed

For months he taught us, stiff-faced.
His old tweed jacket closely buttoned up,
his gestures careful and deliberate.

We didn't understand what he was teaching us.
It was as if a veil, a gauzy bandage, got between
what he was showing us and what we thought we saw.

He had the air of a gardener, fussily protective
of young seedlings, but we couldn't tell
if he was hiding something or we simply couldn't see it.

At first we noticed there were often scraps of leaves
on the floor where he had stood. Later, thin wisps
of thread like spider's web fell from his jacket.

Finally we grew to understand the work. And on that day
he opened his jacket, which to our surprise
seemed lined with patterned fabric of many shimmering
    hues.

Then he smiled and sighed. And with this movement
the lining rippled and instantly the room was filled
with a flickering storm of swirling butterflies.

Dave Calder

Nasty Pets

Deep deep down
where nobody goes,
in teachers' shoes
between their toes.

You'll find blue beetles
and a worm,
with two fat fleas
which like to squirm.

You'll find a maggot
and a snail,
gobbling bits
of old toenail.

You'll find all these,
sucking sweet,
for teachers never
wash their feet.

Andrew Collett

Tall Story

graph

my

on

it

fit

not

could

but

giraffe,

Sir's

measure

to

went

I went to measure Sir's giraffe, but could not fit it on my

Mike Johnson

The Staff

Miss Linnet is neat and very precise.
She flutters her skirts around.
She sweeps along the corridors
thin fingers curled round
her art pad, feet tapping along
in stiletto heels, sharp as tacks.

Mrs Tabby has green eyes.
Be sure they'll find you out.
You may think she is snoozing
curled up in her chair
but one ear is always pricked
to see what you're doing there.

Mr Mastiff's our head.
He's gruff and snappy.
Miss Linnet and Mrs Tabby say
his bark's as bad as his bite.
You'll never get the better of him –
he's always in the right.

Angela Topping

Good for Discipline

Our teacher's got a dinosaur:
She keeps him in her bottom drawer;
He can't get out, he knows the score
 – But, as the silent minutes pass,
You'll hear his muffled dino-roar!

She's shrunk him down to mini-size,
With mini-scales and mini-eyes,
With scary patterns on his thighs
And mini-teeth like spikes of glass,
To bite and tear and terrorise!

She feeds him desks and cloakroom hooks,
She feeds him mice and bats and rooks,
She feeds him smiles and dirty looks,
She feeds him lumps of iron and brass
 – And children who forget their books!

His nature's red in tooth and claw,
With powerful legs and crushing jaw;
His belly drags upon the floor
 – And if you muck about in class,
You'll meet our teacher's dinosaur!

Tony Charles

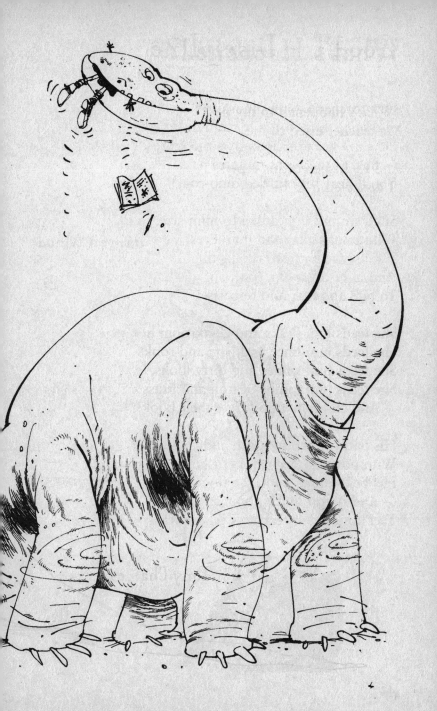

What's Happened?

"What's happened to my pet?"
My teacher cried to me.

And I whispered this reply:
"I dissected it in Biology."

Darren Moody

Miss Smith's Garden Secret

Last Saturday we helped Miss Smith and this is what she said:
"Please do some weeding by the path, *but don't look in the shed*!"

As we dug into the earth, the ground began to quake,
we saw the walls of Miss Smith's shed tremble, wobble, shake.

Clouds of smoke and gusts of fire from underneath the door
scorched our wellies, made them burn until our toes were sore.

"What's in there, miss?" we all yelled, as we dropped our trowels,
then from deep inside the shed came fearsome grunts and growls.

"It's just my pet," she tried to smile, "please don't look inside,"
but with a bang the roof flew off, the door burst open wide.

We didn't know just what we'd see, but thought it would be big,
perhaps a monster or a dragon, but not a guinea pig!

It had a test-tube in each paw, it seemed a bit upset,
"That experiment went wrong," it said, "but I'll perfect it yet."

We come top in Science now, thanks to our secret teacher,
a real Boff, a real Prof, Miss Smith's amazing creature!

David Harmer

Where Teachers Keep their Pets

Mrs Cox has a fox
nesting in her curly locks.

Mr Spratt's tabby cat
sleeps beneath his bobble hat.

Miss Cahoots has various newts
swimming in her zip-up boots.

Mr Spry has Fred his fly
eating food stains from his tie.

Mrs Groat shows off her stoat
round the collar of her coat.

Mr Spare's got grizzly bears
hiding in his spacious flares.

And . . .

Mrs Vickers has a stick insect called "Stickers"
. . . but no one's ever seen where she keeps it.

Paul Cookson

Spelling Bee

Our teacher's got a Spelling Bee
Of which we're very wary.
It sits by itself on our teacher's shelf
Beside her dictionary.

Our teacher's got a Spelling Bee.
It buzzes round your head,
Whenever you make a spelling mistake
And circles the word in red.

Our teacher's got a Spelling Bee.
We treat it with respect.
It brushes your neck as it makes a check
That your spelling is correct.

Our teacher's got a Spelling Bee.
It keeps us on our toes.
Whenever we make a spelling mistake
The Spelling Bee always knows.

Our teacher's got a Spelling Bee
Of which we're very wary.
It sits by itself on our teacher's shelf
Beside her dictionary.

John Foster

Teachers' Pets

Teachers' pets are strange and yet
they seem to do what you'd expect.
Each one has the strangest quirk
reflecting aspects of their work.

Our English teacher's pet just sets
special word games for us.
A tiny type of dinosaur
he's got a small Thesaurus.

Mr Einstein drones so much
in Science we all snore.
His pet looks just like him too
. . . as well as being a boar.

PE's Mr G shows off
and always makes a fuss
when all the sports day team events
are won by his octopus.

Mrs Green is never here,
our class is left alone.
She's got a homing pigeon
that always takes her home.

Mr Sawyer's worried
about his loss of hair.
He's got a chameleon wig
but no one knows it's there.

Our English teacher's wild and
untamed classic stood before us.
Her very literary pet,
Miss Emily's Brontë Saurus

Paul Cookson

Cut Down to Size?

Mr Bumble had a pet –
A massive hairy gorilla,
And he used it to control his class,
He said it was a killer!

No one dared to mess around,
No one dared to mumble,
No one even dared to blink
When taught by Mr Bumble.

Until one day a new boy came,
His name was Brainstorm Ben,
And things would never ever ever
Be the same again.

For on his first day in the class –
A day like any other –
Brainstorm Ben said, "'Scuse me sir,
Is that your younger brother . . . ?"

Clive Webster

It's True

I don't believe yer.
It's true, a big hairy one.

Geroff, you'd hear it.
Some have, screeching at night.

But what does he feed it?
The lines of those kept in at break.

No bird would eat those.
Who said it was a bird?

You did.
No, I never. There's other things

than birds go screeching at night.
It makes its nest in chalk dust.

Now I know you're fibbing.
I'm not, actually.

OK, then, why has no one ever seen it?
Some have, shifting from foot

to foot in the stock cupboard.
Have you?

No. But I dare you to go.
No way. I don't care what

sort of animal that is, there's no way
I'd try and look in that stock cupboard.

You know what Sir's like.
We'd better get these lines done

before the bell goes.
I must not witter on in class.

Angela Topping

My Teacher's Great Big Tropical Fish Tank

My teacher's great big tropical fish tank is huge.
It fills up a whole wall in his classroom.

He changes the water regularly.
It's at exactly the right temperature.

There are pebbles, stones, deep sea wrecks
and sunken treasure chests in the sand.

Plants waft gracefully in the gentle currents
and those little bubbles rise to the surface constantly.

Yes, my teacher's great big tropical fish tank is huge.
It covers up a whole wall in his classroom.

He hasn't got any tropical fish though . . .

Mind you, the guinea pigs seem quite happy.
They like the snorkels, masks and flippers.

Paul Cookson

Our Pet Teacher

Sir's suits are sort of shabby,
grey, wrinkled, big and baggy,
his eyes and nose
all match his clothes,
his lips and ears are saggy.

Sir certainly was never meant
to be a gent who's elegant
but we don't mind
if he's designed
to look more like an elephant.

Gina Douthwaite

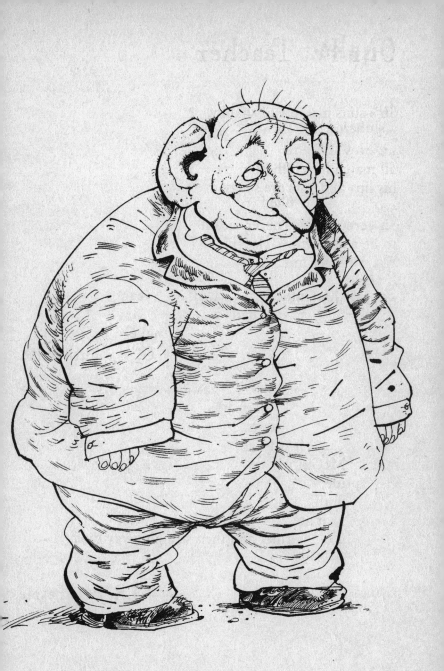

Snake

It
  slithered
      in the
          classroom
              and
            filled
          our
      hearts
    with
  fear,   half our
    Mr McGuffie's   eaten   year.
          viper had   A
                          snake
                            as
                        long
                        as
                    maths
                  tests,
            it was
        McGuffie's
    pride,
      until
        it ate
          a ruler and then straightaway died.

I.R. Eric Petrie

A selected list of poetry books available from Macmillan

The prices shown below are correct at the time of going to press. However, Macmillan Publishers reserve the right to show new retail prices on covers which may differ from those previously advertised.

All Macmillan titles can be ordered at your local bookshop or are available by post from:

**Book Service by Post
PO Box 29, Douglas, Isle of Man IM99 1BQ**

Credit cards accepted. For details:
Telephone: 01624 675137
Fax: 01624 670923
E-mail: bookshop@enterprise.net